THIS WALKER BOOK BELONGS TO:

_____

_____

12

_____ AUG 2015

_____

A 1

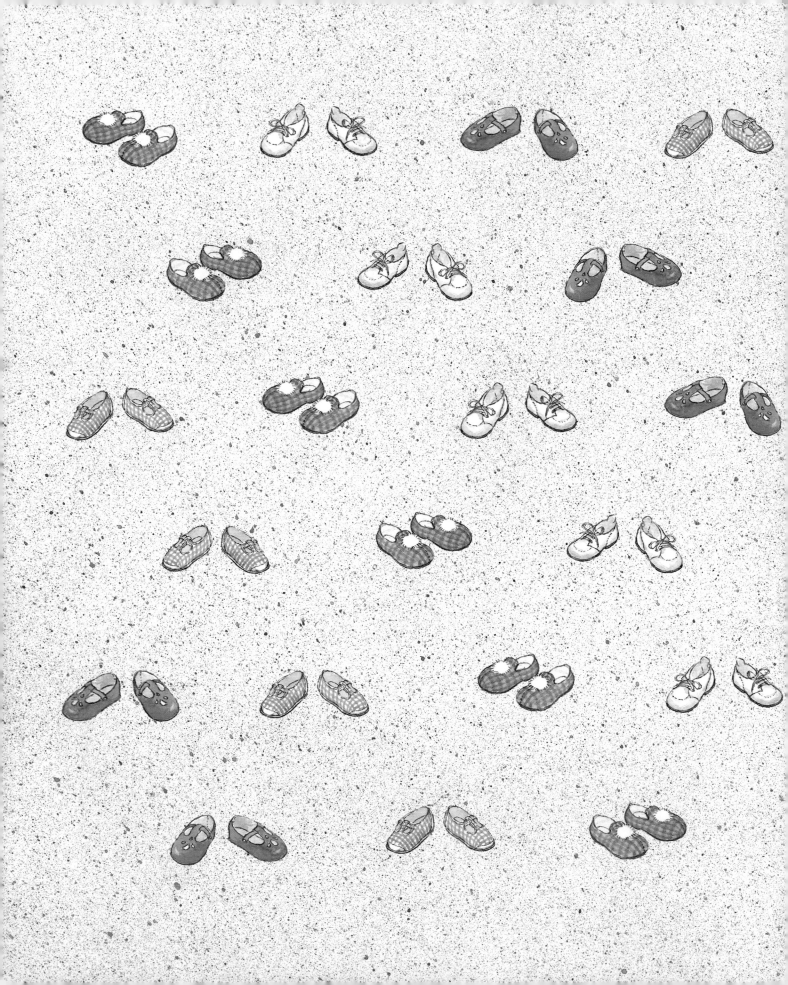

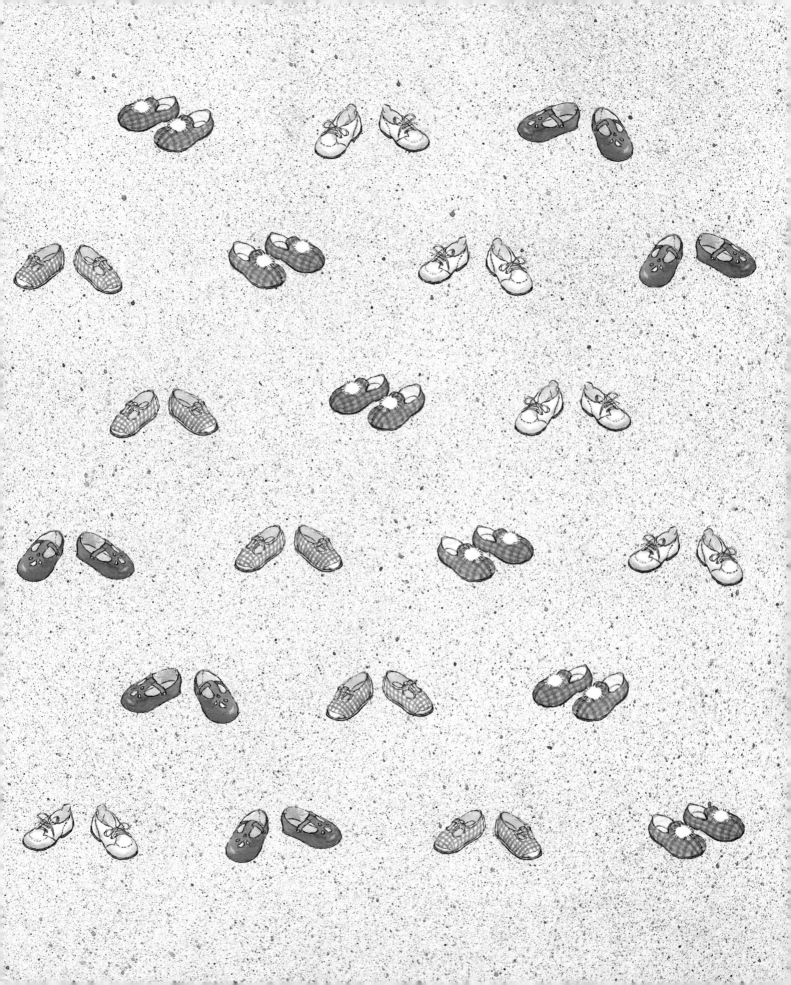

For Mara and Marissa
M.W.

For Sarah, Rowan, Rachel,
Helen, Sarah W. and Charlie…
Giants to be.
P.D.

First published 1989 by Walker Books Ltd
87 Vauxhall Walk, London SE11 5HJ

This edition published 2001

2 4 6 8 10 9 7 5 3 1

Text © 1989 Martin Waddell
Illustrations © 1989 Penny Dale

Printed in Hong Kong

British Library Cataloguing in Publication Data:
a catalogue record for this book
is available from the British Library

ISBN 0-7445-7580-X (hb)
ISBN 0-7445-7836-1 (pb)

Once There Were GIANTS

· · · · · · · · · · · · · ·

MARTIN WADDELL

illustrated by

PENNY DALE

WALKER BOOKS
AND SUBSIDIARIES
LONDON · BOSTON · SYDNEY

Once there were Giants in our house.
There were Mum and Dad and
Jill and John and Uncle Tom.

The small one on the rug is me.

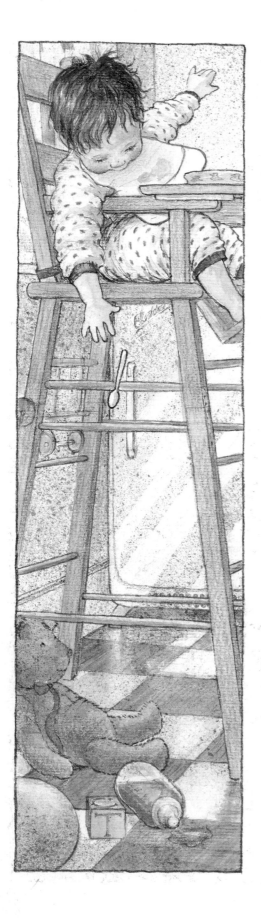

When I could sit up
Mum bought a high chair.
I sat at the table
way up in the sky
with Mum and Dad and
Jill and John and Uncle Tom.

The one throwing porridge is me.

When I could crawl
I crawled round the floor.
Dad was a dragon and
he gave a roar that scared
Jill and John and Uncle Tom.

The one who is crying is me.

When I could walk
I walked to the park with
Jill and John and Uncle Tom.
We fed the ducks and
Jill stood on her head.

The one in the duck pond is me.

When I could talk
I talked and talked!
I annoyed Uncle Tom and
got sat upon by Jill and by John.
That's John on my head
and Jill on my knee.

The one on my bottom is me!

When I could run
I ran and ran,
chased by Mum and Dad
and Uncle Tom and
Jill on her bike and
my brother John.

The one who is puffed out is me.

When I went to playgroup
I wouldn't play games and
I called people names and
upset the water on Millie Magee.
She's the one with the towel.

The one being scolded is me!

When I went to school
I'd got bigger by then.
Mum had to leave at
a quarter to ten and
she didn't come back
for a long, long time.
I didn't shout and
I didn't scream.
She came for me at
a quarter to three.

The one on Mum's knee is me.

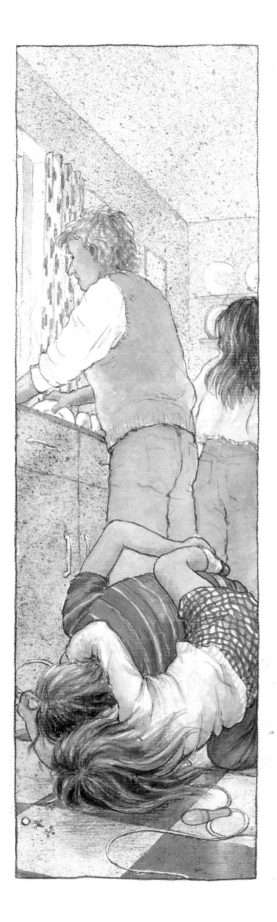

When I went to the top class
I had lots of fun.
I got big and strong
and punched my brother John.
He's the one with the sore nose.

The one with the black eye is me.

When I went to Big School
I was taller than Mum,
and nearly as tall as my Uncle Tom.
But I never caught up
with my brother John.
I ran and I jumped
and they all came to see.
There they are cheering.

The one who's just winning is me.

When I went to work
I lived all by myself.
Then I met Don and we married.
There's Jill and John
and Uncle Tom
and Mum's the one crying,
and Dad is the one
with the beer on his head.

The bride looking happy is me!

Then we had a baby girl
and things changed.

There are Giants in our house again!

There is my husband, Don,
and Jill and John,
my Mum and my Dad
and Uncle Tom
and one of the Giants is…

ME!

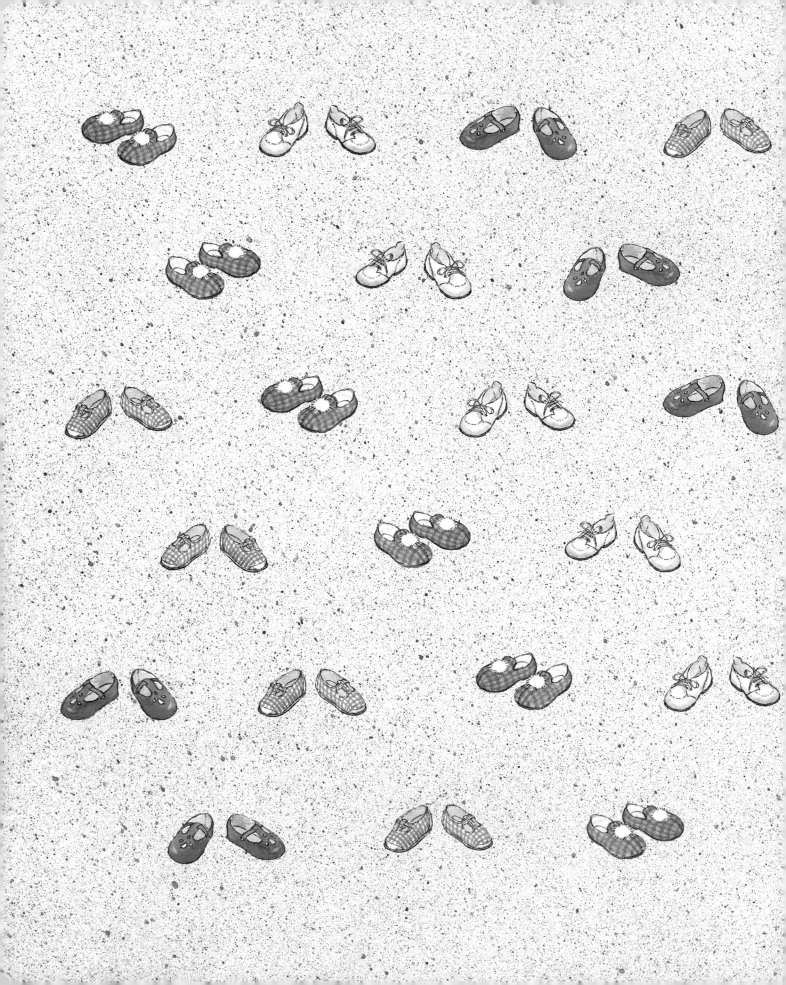

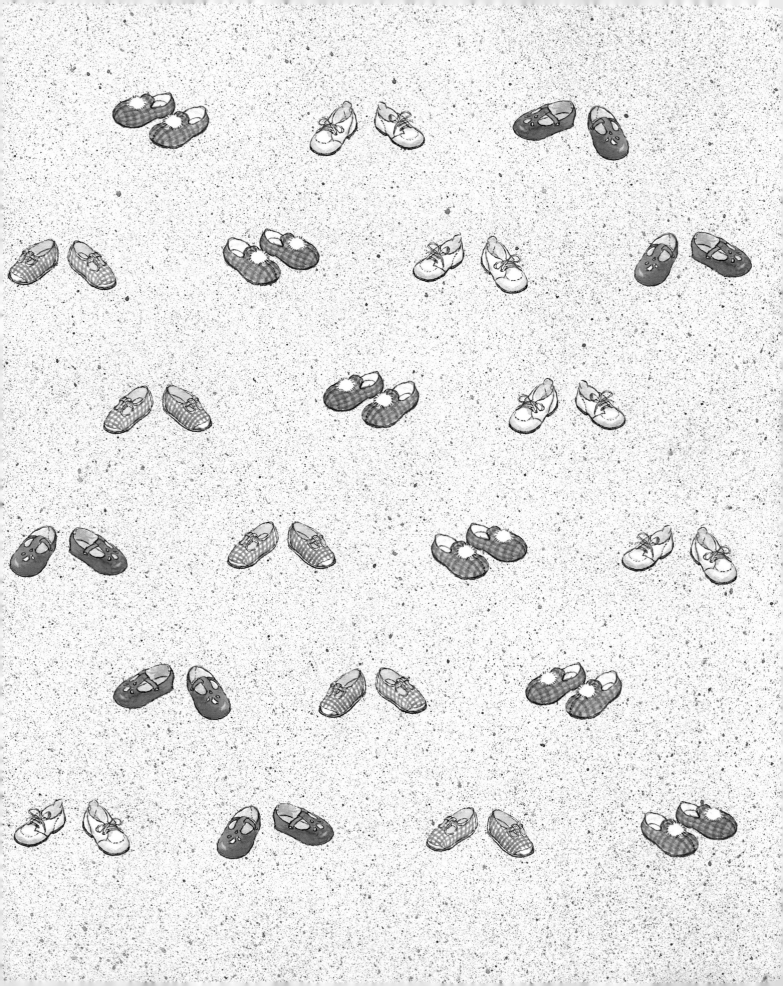

MARTIN WADDELL says of **Once There Were Giants**, "Small children live in a world designed for big people. I wrote this story to help them understand it, and the idea of growing older. It is the simplest of my three 'wheel of life' books, the other two being *The Hidden House* and *The Toymaker*."

Martin Waddell is one of the finest contemporary writers of books for young people. Twice Winner of the Smarties Book Prize – for *Farmer Duck* and *Can't You Sleep, Little Bear?* – he also won the Kurt Maschler Award for *The Park in the Dark* and the Best Books for Babies Award for *Rosie's Babies* (also illustrated by Penny Dale). Among his many other titles are *Owl Babies* and *A Kitten Called Moonlight*. He was the Irish nominee for the 2000 Hans Christian Andersen Award. He lives with his wife Rosaleen in County Down, Northern Ireland.

PENNY DALE asked friends and neighbours to serve as models for the illustrations for this book. "Everyone grows older in the book, so I had to imagine my models for the parents and the uncle twenty years later. When I finished, they all said, 'Oh, so that's how I'm going to look!'"

Penny Dale is one of this country's leading illustrators of children's books. She has illustrated many books for Walker, as well as her own stories, which include *Bet You Can't!*; *Ten in the Bed*; *Ten Out of Bed*; *Ten Play Hide-and-Seek*; *The Elephant Tree*; *Wake Up Mr B!* (Commended for the Kate Greenaway Medal) and *Big Brother, Little Brother*.

Other books by Martin Waddell and Penny Dale

Night Night, Cuddly Bear   0-7445-6780-7 (h/b)   £9.99
Rosie's Babies   0-7445-2335-4 (p/b)   £4.99
When the Teddy Bears Came   0-7445-4763-6 (p/b)   £4.99